Unicorn Dreams

Fulton Books, Inc.
Meadville, PA

Published by Fulton Books 2021

ISBN 978-1-63985-325-0 (paperback)
ISBN 978-1-63985-326-7 (digital)

Printed in the United States of America

Unicorn Dreams

KELLEY MAYS

Abby dreams of having a unicorn of her very own every single day. She and her unicorn will have lots of fun and play!

Her unicorn will be purple with a tail that is pink. Her unicorn will also be as fast as you can blink.

Her unicorn will be as kind as can be and will fly Abby high above the trees.

Her unicorn will sing songs and teach Abby all the words. Then they will sing along together with all the pretty birds.

Her unicorn will stay close to her and never go too
far. They will look up at the sky and wish on a shooting
star.

When bedtime comes, her unicorn will tuck her in tight. With a hug and a kiss, Abby's unicorn will tell her "sweet dreams and good night."

15

About the Author

Kelley Mays is the author of *Unicorn Dreams* and the creator of "The Shabby Mom" blog. A professional in the printing industry by day, a writer by night, she received her bachelor of arts in communication from the University of Cincinnati. She is a Cincinnati native, a lover of dogs, ice cream, and beaches. Currently residing in Monroe, Ohio, she also loves gardening and being a mom to her daughter, Abby.

You can chat with Kelley on Instagram at @kelleymays or visit her online at www.theshabbymom.com.

CPSIA information can be obtained
at www.ICGtesting.com
Printed in the USA
BVHW012107140223
658490BV00014B/1117